DC
SUPER
HEROES

BATMAN

CATWOMAN'S
CLASSROOM OF CLAWS

WRITTEN BY
SCOTT SONNEBORN

ILLUSTRATED BY
DAN SCHOENING

BATMAN CREATED BY
BOB KANE WITH BILL FINGER

Curious Fox
a capstone company-publishers for children

CHAPTER 1

THE FIRST LESSON

"Now, Robin!" whispered Batman.

Robin nodded and crashed through the skylight into the building below. Batman followed, his cape flapping quietly as he fell through the air and landed by his partner's side.

The two heroes were in the 4th Street Library. Together, they peered around the edge of a bookshelf. Four criminals in black masks and costumes surrounded an elderly librarian. She was the only one left in the small library this late at night.

"This is a robbery!" shouted the tallest crook. "Put your hands down!"

The librarian looked at him, confused.

One of the other crooks tapped the tall one on the shoulder. "Wait, shouldn't that be 'put your hands *up*?'" he asked.

"Uh, right," said the tall criminal sheepishly. "What he said."

Robin gave Batman a look. There was something different about these crooks.

"Give us all the money," the tall crook ordered the librarian.

"Money?" replied the librarian. "This is a library. We lend out books for free. The only money we have is from late fines." The librarian opened a box on the counter. Inside was a small pile of coins.

Robin shot Batman another look that said, *What kind of crook would rob a place that doesn't have any money?*

There was no time to worry about that now, though. Batman gave Robin the signal. Time to go to work.

WHAM! Robin's bo-staff knocked the tall crook off of his feet and bounced him off a shelf of books. He hit the floor hard.

At the same time, Batman threw a Batarang. **ZING!** It pinned another crook to the wall by his shirt.

The last two crooks were standing near the rear exit. Robin knew that just beyond that door was a busy street. He had been in this library many times to study. When he wasn't fighting crime with Batman, Robin was Tim Drake, a secondary school pupil.

If the crooks made it out to the street, Batman and Robin might lose them in the traffic. Instead of running for it, though, the crooks charged right at Batman.

Robin couldn't believe it. *Unless you're the Joker or Mr Freeze, you've got no chance against Batman,* thought Robin. *That's something every criminal in Gotham City knows, except these guys. They don't seem to know the first thing about being crooks!*

As Batman wrapped up the last of the crooks, Robin went back and checked on the one he had taken down with his bo-staff. He was out cold. Robin searched his pockets. Inside he found an application to a school . . . for future villains! The school didn't have a name or an address. The flyer just read, "You email us. We'll find you."

No wonder these guys made so many mistakes! realized Robin. *They weren't real criminals at all. At least, not yet. They were students learning how to be crooks!*

Robin ran up to Batman and showed him the flyer.

"A school for criminals?" said Batman as he read the pamphlet.

Robin nodded. "I guess these guys were here on some kind of field trip," he said.

"They're not the only ones," Batman said. He pointed to his mask. There was an earpiece hidden inside that picked up the police radio. Other classes of student criminals were on "field trips" all over Gotham. One was robbing a medical supply company. Another was at the Jewellery Exchange.

"What are we waiting for?" cried Robin. "Let's go and teach these student crooks a lesson!"

Robin started for the door, but Batman stopped him.

"No," said Batman. "The police are reporting classes popping up all over Gotham on 'field trips.' We can't chase after them all. We have to be cleverer than that."

He's right, thought Robin. *No surprise there. He's Batman. He's pretty much always right.*

"To shut down this school," Batman continued, "we have to find out who is running it. And there's only one way to do that." Batman gave Robin a look. "I think it's time for you to go to school."

CHAPTER 2

CRIME SCHOOL

Later that night, Batman raced around Gotham City in the Batmobile, hunting down more student villains on "field trips." Tim Drake was at an Internet cafe filled with computer gamers. All around him, kids were playing video games.

The game Tim was playing was more dangerous. He was about to go undercover as a student villain. That's why Tim was in his street clothes and using the cafe's computer. He didn't want anyone to know it was really Robin applying to the school.

Tim typed in the email address he had found on the flyer and hit the Send button. His application was on its way. All he could do now was wait and see if the school fell for his trick.

About an hour later, he felt a hand on his shoulder. Tim looked up and saw someone wearing the same mask and costume as the student crooks in the library.

"Put this on," the stranger said, handing Tim a blindfold.

Apparently, his application had been accepted.

Moments later, Tim could feel and hear that he was in a moving car. Thanks to the blindfold, though, he had no idea where he was going.

Tim didn't know what he would find when he got to the school. Would he have a place to hide his things? He didn't know, so he couldn't risk bringing any bat-gear. If anything went wrong, Tim had no way of contacting Batman. Until Tim cracked the case, he was on his own.

When the blindfold came off, Tim got his first view of the school. He was in a small, windowless room with a big, mean-looking older boy staring at him.

"Hey, how's it going?" Tim said, trying to be friendly and fit in. "I just got here."

"Do I look like I care?" growled the boy. He held up a costume and a mask. The other boys were already wearing the outfit. It was the same one worn by the student crooks in the library. "That's your school uniform. Put it on!"

"Uh, thanks," Tim said as he put on the costume and mask. "So, what's your name?" Tim asked, giving it one more try.

"Shut up," snarled the boy.

"Really?" Tim replied with a smile. "That's a weird name, but it's nice to meet you, Shut Up."

The look the boy gave Tim told the young hero that he was on thin ice, and that the ice had already begun to crack.

So much for fitting in, thought Tim. *This is worse than my first day at secondary school!*

Then a skinny kid came into the room, and Shut Up left without saying goodbye.

"I'd watch out for him," said the skinny kid as he held out his hand. "My name is the Food Fighter. That's not my real name, of course. It's my villain name. Cool, huh?"

"I'm here to give you a tour of the school," the Food Fighter continued. "I always volunteer to give new kids their tours." Then he added in a whisper, "It's a great way to get out of going to PE."

He opened a door that led to a long corridor. As they walked down the hall, Tim was surprised to see that crime school was pretty much just like his own school.

Well, *pretty much.*

There were lockers in the corridor with combination locks. The pupils were using them to practice lock picking.

Next to the lockers was a classroom. Tim poked his head inside and saw what looked like a technical lesson. The pupils were hard at work on a car – learning how to steal it.

"Attention!" crackled a voice over a loudspeaker. "The next lesson begins in two minutes." The voice belonged to a woman. It sounded familiar, but Tim couldn't quite place it.

"That's the Head Teacher," said the Food Fighter, answering Tim's question before he could ask. "She's the boss of the school."

Bingo! Just the person Tim was looking for. "I'd like to meet her," he said.

"Good luck," said the Food Fighter. "Only the top pupils get invited to her office."

Now I know what I have to do to crack the case, thought Tim. *Get to the head of the class.* He looked around at his competition. Most of the young crooks were large, and they outnumbered Tim by 100 to 1.

This isn't going to be easy, he realized.

After passing five or six classrooms, Tim and the Food Fighter arrived at the end of the windowless corridor.

"And last but not least," announced the Food Fighter, "the most important room in the school."

Tim wondered what was inside. A weapons lab? The vault where they stash all their stolen loot?

The Food Fighter opened the door, and Tim saw the canteen. It was exactly like every canteen in every school Tim had ever attended. In other words, it was loud, rowdy, and the food smelled awful.

Tim soon found out why such a skinny kid was called the Food Fighter, though. He started eating while he was still in line.

Tim couldn't imagine anyone eating faster than that. Until they sat down, that is, and the Food Fighter was able to dive into his tray with both hands. About half the food ended up in his mouth. The rest of it landed on Tim.

Note to self, thought Tim. *Never eat lunch next to a guy who calls himself the Food Fighter!*

"So, what do you call yourself?" asked the Food Fighter, as he scoffed down his burger. Then he helped himself to Tim's chips.

"Rob –" Tim stopped short. *How could I be so stupid!* He moaned to himself. *The sight of those half-chewed chips slurping around in the Food Fighter's mouth must have short-circuited my brain for a second! I almost blew my cover!*

The Food Fighter gave Tim a look. Tim could just imagine what he was thinking: *What kind of villain gives himself a name like Rob? What's next – a villain named Joe or Eugene? Something's not right.*

Tim had to think of something quick. But before he could, the Food Fighter suddenly smiled and said, "Oh, wait, I get it. You're called 'Rob' because you like to rob people. Great name!"

Whew! Time to change the subject. "So where do you think we are?" Tim asked.

"We're in the canteen," the Food Fighter replied. "I thought you would have worked that out." He swallowed another big gulp of Tim's lunch as if to prove the point.

"No, I mean, where do you think the school is located?" Tim said.

The Food Fighter looked at Tim like he had just asked the stupidest question in the history of questions.

"Why would they blindfold us if they wanted us to know that?" he said.

Tim decided to drop the subject. They were obviously in a warehouse. But where? There were no windows. *I'll have to find a way to sneak outside and –*

"Hey, you two!" a voice called out. Tim looked up. It was Shut Up.

"We have names," replied the Food Fighter. "Mine's Food Fighter and his is –"

"Do I look like I care?" barked Shut Up. "You two get to room four. You're late for PE."

Sneaking out of the school will have to wait, Tim told himself.

In the meantime, Tim hoped that PE might be fun. PE was always one of the highlights of Tim's day at Gotham Secondary School. *Besides,* he thought, *I could use some exercise after watching the Food Fighter eat all of that food!*

Tim looked at the Food Fighter. For the first time since he had sat down, the Food Fighter had stopped eating. His mouth just hung open.

"Why've you stop chewing?" Tim asked.

"I've lost my appetite," the Food Fighter said, looking down at his tray sadly.

"Why?" Tim asked.

"Didn't you hear him?" sputtered the Food Fighter. "We've got to go to PE!"

Tim began to think he might be in trouble.

CHAPTER 3

THE PE LESSON

Oomph! Yes, he was definitely in trouble. Tim picked himself up from where Shut Up had thrown him to the floor. This PE lesson wasn't like any Tim had ever had. It was a combination of a martial arts dojo, an ultimate fighting cage match, and a football practice.

Shut Up had picked Tim to be the tackling dummy.

The Food Fighter helped Tim to his feet. "I'd like to hit that guy with a pie," whispered the Food Fighter.

"I feel the same way," moaned Tim, rubbing his arm. It was numb from the beating he'd just taken. "Or I would feel the same way if I could feel anything."

"Let's go again," ordered Shut Up, beckoning Tim back for another round. Shut Up hadn't even broken a sweat. He smiled, confident that he was about to thrash Tim into tomorrow.

Tim crouched low, trying to create as small a target as possible. Shut Up was obviously well trained in the martial arts, but he hadn't been trained by Batman!

Shut Up swung his fist. Tim dived low, knocking Shut Up's feet out from under him. When the older boy's chin hit the floor, he was surprised – and angry. Shut Up growled, and a half dozen of his friends helped him to his feet, glaring at Tim.

Tim wasn't afraid of one bully – but seven? Could he handle that many? It looked like he was about to find out. Shut Up led his friends right up to Tim.

"Stop!" said the Head Teacher over the loudspeaker. "I've seen enough. This class is ready to go on its first field trip."

All the pupils, including Tim, let out a big cheer. Tim knew he had probably just avoided being clobbered. More importantly, this was his chance to find out where the school was located. All he had to do was keep his eyes open when the class left the school.

For the first time since Tim arrived, he had got a break. Then Shut Up handed him a blindfold. "Put it on!" he shouted.

So much for that idea.

Moments later, Tim was back inside the van, or at least that's what he thought. He hadn't seen anything since being blindfolded.

SKKRREEEE Suddenly, he heard brakes slamming to a stop. Then a door opened. Someone ripped off Tim's blindfold and gave him a push.

Tim's eyes adjusted to the light, and he saw that the van was parked in front of the Gotham shopping centre. The Food Fighter was there, and so were Shut Up and the rest of the pupils from PE.

Tim turned to see the van roar off. "Wait!" he yelled. "How will we get back to school?"

"They'll come back and get us," said the Food Fighter, "if we steal enough."

The other pupils were already charging into the shopping centre. The Food Fighter took off after them.

"C'mon!" he called back to Tim. "Time to show off what we've learned!"

Tim was in a tough spot. He didn't want to steal, but he didn't want to blow his cover either. He still didn't know where the school was located. If he was going to crack this case, he had to complete this "field trip" and get back to school.

As Tim pushed through the glass doors of the shopping centre, he saw there was no use worrying about having to steal. In fact, there was no way anyone in the class was going to steal anything.

Because standing right in front of them was . . . Batman!

CHAPTER 4

THE FIELD TRIP

WHAM! Shut Up fell to the ground as Batman's Batarang bounced off him.

Tim couldn't help but smile.

Batman turned and ran towards Tim. Tim's smile immediately disappeared. He remembered he was wearing his crime school costume and mask like all of the other young criminals.

Batman had no idea he was Robin! He thought Tim was just another crook to take down.

Tim had always known that crooks were afraid of Batman. As the Dark Knight barrelled towards him, he finally knew *why*.

Tim froze.

All Tim had to do was yell out, "It's me, Robin!" But that would blow his cover. His investigation would be over. He'd never find out where the crime school was located or who was in charge.

If Tim didn't, though, Batman would clobber him. He had to think of something to say to tip-off Batman without giving away his identity to the crooks.

With Batman's hand just inches away from his face, Tim suddenly realized, *It doesn't matter what I say!* All he had to do was say something. Batman would recognize his voice.

"Hey, Bats!" Tim shouted. "You're not so tough."

All the young crooks stared at Tim. *I think that impressed them,* he thought. Even more importantly – it worked. Batman gave Tim the tiniest of nods. He knew!

Batman continued towards Tim, but slowly enough that Tim could easily dodge to the side. When he did, Batman crashed hard to the ground as if he had been body slammed.

Tim wasn't expecting that to happen. Without even thinking, Tim reached out to help Batman up. Batman flopped backwards as if Tim had punched him. That's when Tim understood what was going on. Batman was making it look like Tim was fighting him and winning!

As Batman and Tim continued their fake battle, Tim looked over at his classmates. They were all staring at him wide-eyed, in awe. Even Shut Up looked at Tim like he was the coolest kid ever. Tim couldn't help but show off a little. It wasn't like he was ever going to get another chance to beat Batman in a fight!

Then Batman grabbed Tim's collar and pulled him to the floor. *I guess he's trying to make sure the fight looks convincing,* thought Tim. *But that was a little too convincing.*

By the time Tim got to his feet, Batman was gone. All of the young villains were treating Tim like a hero. He had made it to the head of the class!

Back at the school, Shut Up took off Tim's blindfold and pointed to a door.

Tim opened it. There she was, sitting behind her desk. Tim couldn't believe it! The Head Teacher was . . .

CHAPTER 5

HEAD TEACHER

Catwoman!

"I've chosen you to be my school's student council," she told Tim and the other kids who had gathered in her office. "You are now the leaders of my student body. Tonight, you will lead all of them out into the city to rob Gotham blind. Once you fan out into the streets, not even Batman will be able stop you all."

"Speaking of Batman," she went on, "I have to give him some credit. He was the one who inspired this school."

"It seems like every time I try to steal something," Catwoman continued, "Batman and that runt Robin find a way to beat me. Well, if working with one teenage sidekick helps him that much, I thought I'd see how much more I could do with 100 teenage sidekicks!"

Hearing that made Tim's blood boil. *Sidekick?!* he screamed to himself. *I'm Batman's partner, not his sidekick. How hard is that for people to remember?*

Catwoman unfolded a map on her desk. The places she wanted to rob were circled on it. Arrows showed the path each group of pupils would take to their target.

Tim searched for any sign of the school. It wasn't marked on the map, but all the arrows started in the same place. *That has to be where the school is located!*

The map was the key to breaking the case. All Tim had to do was quietly slip it into his pocket while everyone was looking at Catwoman. He decided to take a chance.

"You think you can steal from a thief?" hissed Catwoman. Tim felt her hand grip his wrist like a claw. "I don't know what you had in mind by trying to take that map, but you've made a very big mistake."

Everyone in the room, including Shut Up, grabbed on to Tim. "Head Teacher should have let me and my mates finish you off back in PE," Shut Up said, cracking his knuckles. "Better late than never, I suppose."

All Tim could think was that the next thing that happened to him would probably be the last thing that ever happened to him.

BOOM!

An explosion rocked the room! A wall fell down, and Batman rushed in through the smoke and dust.

Catwoman and the young crooks were shocked, but no one was more surprised than Tim!

How did he know where I was? Tim almost said out loud. *I know, I know, he's Batman. But even Batman has limits. He's not a mind reader.*

Then Tim remembered when Batman had grabbed his collar at the shopping centre. Tim reached inside his shirt and found a Bat-tracker! *Man, is he good!* Tim thought.

"Stunner!" yelled Batman. Tim hit the ground, just as he had done during the thousands of times he had practised this move in the Batcave. Batman released the stunner, a sonic screech that brought everyone who was standing to their knees.

Catwoman had been quick enough to hit the ground. She crawled out of the room as Batman tackled what was left of her student council.

Tim knew he had to stop Catwoman. If she got away, she'd just start another crime school somewhere else, maybe somewhere he and Batman couldn't find. Tim wasn't going to let that happen.

Tim chased her into the corridor. He was gaining on her. Then Shut Up popped up right front of him.

"We've got some unfinished business," the older boy growled.

Tim didn't have time to waste.

Tim took Shut Up down with a single karate kick.

Tim quickly turned to face his next opponent, but Catwoman was prepared. Her razor-like claws were out and ready to strike. Tim thought he was doomed.

Then suddenly, a gob of white mush splattered on Catwoman's face.

"What is this?" the villain cried in confusion.

As Catwoman cleared the mush from her eyes, Tim looked around for the culprit. On the other side of the room, he spotted the Food Fighter, holding a cooking pot and a large wooden spoon.

"Mashed potatoes!" the Food Fighter said, licking a lump from the spoon. "Did you know they're my favourite?" He dug out another spoonful of mashed potatoes.

Then he flung the spuds towards the Catwoman's face.

"Ah!" she cried out again, wiping more mashed potatoes from her eyes. "I can't see!"

Tim quickly tackled Catwoman to the ground. Batman rushed in and wrapped her up for the police. Tim could already hear their sirens in the distance.

"This can't be happening!" Catwoman screamed at Batman. "You show up without Robin, and then you beat me thanks to some other scrawny teenager!"

She glared at Tim, but he couldn't help but smile. *I know she didn't mean to*, he thought, *but she just paid me an awfully big compliment.*

As Batman led Catwoman towards the sound of the sirens, Tim turned and thanked the Food Fighter.

"You know," said the Food Fighter. "I'm actually kind of looking forward to going back to my old school. There are a lot of things I've missed about it – like maths, English, and pizza day."

"I'm glad to hear it," said Tim, "because this school is out . . . for good!"

Published by Curious Fox, an imprint of Capstone Global Library Limited,
– Registered company number: 6695582

www.curious-fox.com

First published by Stone Arch Books in 2010
First published in hardback in the United Kingdom in 2010
Paperback edition first published in the United Kingdom in 2010
The moral rights of the proprietor have been asserted.

Art Director: Bob Lentz
Designer: Bob Lentz
UK Editor: Vaarunika Dharmapala
Originated by Capstone Global Library Ltd
Printed and bound in China

ISBN 978-1-78202-720-1 (paperback)

British Library Cataloguing in Publication Data
A full catalogue record for this book is available from the British Library.